COMMANDER IN CHEESE

Oval Office Escape

Read all the Commander in Cheese adventures!

COMMANDER IN CHEESE

Oval Office Escape

2

Lindsey Leavitt • illustrated by A. G. Ford

A STEPPING STONE BOOK™

Random House 🏠 New York

Photo permissions: pg. 86–91 President portraits from the collection of the Library of Congress Prints and Photographs Division online at www.loc.gov, pg. 93 Socks photo from the collection of the National Archives online at www.archives.gov, pg. 95 JFK image © AP Photo/Look Magazine, pg. 96 Obama image from the collection of the White House online at www.wikimedia.org, pg. 98–99 Situation Room images © United States Government Works

Visit us on the Web!
SteppingStonesBooks.com
randomhousekids.com

Educators and librarians, for a variety of teaching tools,
visit us at RHTeachersLibrarians.com

Library of Congress Cataloging-in-Publication Data
Names: Leavitt, Lindsey, author. | Ford, AG, illustrator.
Title: The Oval Office escape / Lindsey Leavitt ; illustrated by AG Ford.
Description: New York : Random House, [2016] | Series: Commander in Cheese ;
2 | "A Stepping Stone Book." | Summary: "When Ava and Dean are sent to bring lunch to the mice who work in the Situation Room, they discover that the president's cat, Clover, is going to be spending a lot of time in the West Wing"—Provided by publisher.
Identifiers: LCCN 2015027157 | ISBN 978-1-101-93115-8 (paperback) | ISBN 978-1-101-93116-5 (hardcover library binding) | ISBN 978-1-101-93117-2 (ebook)
Subjects: | CYAC: Mice—Fiction. | Brothers and sisters—Fiction. | Presidents—Family—Fiction. | White House (Washington, D.C.)—Fiction. | Humorous stories. | BISAC: JUVENILE FICTION / Animals / Mice, Hamsters, Guinea Pigs, etc. | JUVENILE FICTION / People & Places / United States / General. | JUVENILE FICTION / Humorous Stories.
Classification: LCC PZ7.L46553 Ov 2016 | DDC [E]—dc23
LC record available at http://lccn.loc.gov/2015027157

Printed in the United States of America
10 9 8 7 6 5 4 3 2 1

This book has been officially leveled by using the
F&P Text Level Gradient™ Leveling System.

Random House Children's Books supports the
First Amendment and celebrates the right to read.

To Uncle Kyle, the patron saint of literacy

★ ★ ★ ★ ★ ★ ★ ★ ★

Why do humans love dogs so much? If a
dog runs into a room, a human smiles.
If a mouse runs into a room, a human jumps on
the couch. What's a little mouse going to do?
It's silly.

Plus, dogs aren't smart. Here's a list of rea-
sons why:

1. They need animal trainers! Dogs have to
   learn how to be dogs. Mice don't need
   trainers. Mice know how to be mice.
2. Dogs have stinky breath. It's not their

fault, but what do they do to fix that? Nothing. They open their smelly mouths to breathe, bark, or eat. It's gross.

3. Dogs need to be potty trained. POTTY TRAINED.

4. Dogs chase cars. Guess what, dogs? You're not going to catch that car. Ever!

But even though dogs aren't smart, mice like them. Dogs leave mice alone. When President Obama lived in the White House, he had two dogs: Bo and Sunny. The Squeakertons, the mouse family that has lived in the White House for over two hundred years, hardly ever saw those dogs. Same with Miss Beazley, Spot, Barney, Buddy . . . the list is very long. White House dogs spend their days chewing on bones or barking at squirrels. Mice like it that way.

Dogs are really only smart when it comes to *one thing*. Dogs chase cats. And everyone knows how mice feel about cats. Cats might be smart, but they're also rude. And spoiled. And dangerous. Cats are the worst.

Cats eat mice. House cats, country cats . . . No mouse is safe. Cats are fed big meals by their owners. They still chase after mice in their basements, backyards, and barns.

It just isn't right.

Anyway, this story isn't about dogs, or even cats. It's about Ava and Dean Squeakerton. Dean is nine, and Ava is seven.

The president doesn't know about Ava and Dean, but her kids do. Hopefully, they won't tell anyone about the mice. The kids *seem* nice, but I'm sure dogs *seem* smart to some humans.

Today is President Caroline Abbey's first day at work. Her office, the Oval Office, is in the West Wing of the White House. Her staff is new too. It's a very busy day. A day that should not include mice.

But it does. Thanks to a c-a-t who was the biggest diva to ever enter the White House!

Just a regular, same old, normal Saturday. Ava and Dean were still tired from a wild adventure the night before. They would catch up on reading or maybe take relaxing baths.

But first, they stopped in the kitchen for breakfast. The mouse kitchen is built in the wall of the main White House kitchen. The cook, Libby, filled two bowls with one Cheerio each. One Cheerio was the perfect mouse-sized snack.

"I want to see if we can find note cards," Ava said. "They make strong paper airplanes."

"Or playing cards. We can build a tower with those too," Dean said, eating fast.

"Sounds fun. We have the whole day to play!" Ava said.

Libby pointed to their empty bowls. "Put those in the sink. Oh! And Gregory needs your help with something."

"Gregory?" Dean moaned. "He isn't going to tell us about the history of a White House toilet for three hours again, is he?"

"No, he isn't," Gregory said from the doorway.

Ava and Dean jumped. Even though he was a big mouse, Gregory sometimes snuck up on them. Gregory was a Secret Service mouse. He was in charge of making sure Ava and Dean stayed safe.

"I need you to help bring some food to the West Wing," Gregory said. "We gave the kitchen staff the morning off. They might still be sleeping. Don't wake them up."

"We're in the kitchen," Ava said. "How could we do that from here?"

They knew Gregory liked to give warnings, even about things that didn't need a warning.

Libby handed Gregory and the kids mouse-packs. The packs were loaded with cheese, fruit, bread, and crackers.

"Thank you, Libby," Gregory said. "That bow looks very pretty on you."

Libby touched her bow and blushed. "Oh, Gregory. Such a charmer."

Dean and Ava rolled their eyes. Adults could be so weird.

The mice scurried along the

tunnel built under the West Wing colonnade. "Colonnade" is a fancy word for a sidewalk with columns. This tunnel was a long one. Pictures of past Squeakertons lined the walls. Ava liked the one of Great-Great-Great-(add forty-six more "Greats")-Uncle Brett. He built a mouse airplane like the Wright brothers. Sadly, a bird ate Uncle Brett as soon as he made it into the air. Poor Uncle Brett.

"Your aunt Agnes has been so busy," Gregory said. "Nobody in the Situation Room has slept."

Dean stopped running. "What? We're going to the Situation Room? I've only been there once with our parents."

"Me too!" Ava said. "They don't let little mice in there."

"Not usually," Gregory said. "But this is just

for a bit. Do not touch anything. Do not talk to the busy mice. Do not make a mess. Do not . . ."

Ava and Dean stopped listening to Gregory's "do nots."

The Situation Room is a real room on the ground floor of the West Wing. This is where the president meets other important people to make very important decisions about the country. There is a large table and cushy office chairs. TV screens are everywhere.

That's all I can tell you. It is a TOP-SECRET room where TOP-SECRET stuff happens.

The mice had smaller rooms built into the walls of big White House rooms. The mouse Situation Room looked like the human one. Mice in military uniforms sat at the table, drinking tea. Aunt Agnes also worked in the mouse Situation Room. She dressed differently

than other mice. Today she wore overalls and sandals. Sometimes she colored her ears purple.

Aunt Agnes was a computer wizard. She could fix anything. She set up microphones for the Squeakerton radio broadcast. She wired electricity in the main mouse area. She could probably make world peace if humans ever bothered to listen to animals.

Aunt Agnes waved. "Oh, good. We're all starving. This is so nice."

Dean unpacked a piece of blue cheese. Humans think blue cheese is stinky. Mice think it smells better than roses. "We didn't have any plans today. We're happy to help."

"Well, we were going to build a paper airplane," Ava said. She loved to fly, and Dean loved to build. They were a good brother-and-sister team.

"Just as long as you stay out of trouble." Gregory stacked some berries and bread onto the table. "That should be enough food for everyone."

"We just never know what to expect when a new president starts," Aunt Agnes explained. "We heard she's already having a meeting in the Oval Office."

"Do you think she'll be a nice president?" Ava asked.

"Nice isn't a problem. I just like clean and organized. Humans can be dirty animals," Aunt Agnes said.

"Can we watch the meeting?" Dean asked.

Gregory snorted. "Of course not. The Oval Office is the most famous office in the country. We don't enter when there are humans around."

Gregory ruined fun before it even started. In fact, ruining fun *was* fun for Gregory.

"Well, we're going to make paper airplanes, then," Ava said. "Bye, Gregory."

A soft alarm started to beep. A red ceiling light blinked. The nine mice sitting at the table jumped out of their seats.

A white mouse burst into the room. He was shaking from head to tail. "We have a situation!"

"Of course. This is the *Situation* Room," Aunt Agnes said.

"No. This is serious. It has to do with a"— the mouse lowered his voice—"a . . . c-a-t!"

Cats have always been a "situation" for mice. In the history of the White House, thirty-seven Squeakertons have died because a cat was hungry. But there hadn't been a big cat problem since President George W. Bush's black cat, India. She lived until she was eighteen.

The new president had a cat named Clover. Ava and Dean already had a close call with Clover. They didn't want to see Clover ever again.

"We knew about the cat," Agnes said. Not many mice had the courage to say the c-a-t word. "That's why we were excited to get a video camera. So we can keep an eye on her."

She tapped a wall. A screen came down from the ceiling. Ava and Dean couldn't believe it!

A map of the White House appeared on the screen.

"We have video cameras in a few rooms, but not all of them," Aunt Agnes said. "So we won't know where the cat is all the time. We have to track her movements. Usually the pets stay on the second floor."

The white mouse hopped from one foot to the other. "But . . . but . . . that's not going to matter today!"

"Yes it will." Aunt Agnes smiled at the worried mouse. She was very good at looking calm. "We'll watch Clover for a few days. Then we'll write a schedule and make sure we stay out of her space. We don't need to worry about the cat. A dog would've been better, of course. But we can handle Clover."

"No! Listen!" the white mouse exclaimed. "The c-a-t is in the Oval Office right now."

Gregory frowned. "Pets don't come in the West Wing. We're safe here."

"The c-a-t is visiting the president." The white mouse shook so hard that Ava wondered if he was cold or scared.

"Why would she do that?" Dean asked.

Aunt Agnes pressed a button on a remote. The screen changed from the map to a video shot. It was very low to the ground, but Ava could tell it was the Oval Office. The camera was probably in a mouse hole.

They could see furniture and lots of shoes. When a human moved, they saw the new president. She was holding Clover. The cat smiled like it was the best day ever.

"Oh boy," Dean said.

Aunt Agnes turned up the volume.

"Thank you for coming," President Abbey said.

There were photographers in the room. The president's children, Banks and Macey, were there too. Everyone buzzed with excitement.

"Today is a special day in the White House. My new staff starts work. You will meet my chief of staff soon. But the real boss here is Clover. Say hi, Clover." The president waved a paw for Clover. The photographers laughed and took her picture.

The mice shook their heads as they watched. Seriously, why do humans think cats and dogs are so special when mice are much smarter? And cuter?!

"Clover is my lucky charm. She'll work with me in the Oval Office every day."

Clover hopped out of the president's arms and onto the desk.

"Looks like she is ready to work!" said a photographer.

Clover meowed and curled into a ball. More pictures were snapped.

The president's kids stepped back from the group. They were right in front of the mouse-hole camera.

Banks sighed. "Clover loves the attention."

"She lets you know what she wants," Macey said. "That just means she's strong."

"Except she's a diva! It's all about Clover, all the time," Banks said.

"No. Remember when we went skiing in Vermont?" Macey asked. "You were so wet, and Clover still cuddled with you."

"She bumped me into the snowbank. And she wasn't cuddling—she was begging for food."

"So Clover likes to have things her way. There's nothing wrong with that." Macey walked back to the photographers.

"Yes there is," her brother grumbled. "That cat thinks this is *her* house. It's not. It's America's house!"

Now the mice could see the president again. The president was still talking about her pet. "Clover is also my bodyguard. She will protect the area from bugs and other vermin."

Clover yowled. She stretched. She posed.

Aunt Agnes frowned. "I don't like when humans call us vermin."

"This isn't good," Ava said.

"Really bad," Dean said.

"We're building a large living space for Clover right here," President Abbey said.

Men came in carrying all sorts of furniture. They held up a cat bed, a scratching post, a climbing gym, a water tray, and a golden litter box.

"Fancy furniture," Ava said.

"And heavy," Gregory said. "That gym takes two humans to move."

The movers walked toward the video screen.

Dean stepped back. "They're getting close!"

The screen went black. The gym was blocking the camera!

Aunt Agnes groaned. "Our hidden mouse hole is there too! Now we won't know anything going on in the Oval Office. This is going to mess up our entire network!"

"Thank you for coming to Clover's first photo shoot." The mice could still hear the president's voice, even if they couldn't see anything. "There will be many more. Clover is America's new favorite animal! Now, follow me. I want a picture of Clover in every room of the West Wing."

Aunt Agnes shut off the screens. She sat down at the table. She looked very, very tired.

"Just what we need. A cat walking the hallways when we have work to do." She smiled at her niece and nephew. "Thank you for the food. I have to get busy fixing this now. If it can be fixed."

Dean pointed with his tail. "Gregory is super strong! Let's send him to move the furniture."

Gregory backed away. "Hold on! There is a c-a-t in that room, plus humans. Lots of humans."

"That's right," Ava said. "And trust me. A human can be just as scary as a c-a-t."

"We don't have a choice," Aunt Agnes said. "Contact Mr. Squeakerton."

They called Mr. Squeakerton. Ava and Dean's dad was in charge of the mice in the White House. He was sort of the mouse president.

"James Squeakerton here."

Aunt Agnes told him everything that had happened. Mr. Squeakerton sighed. "Ava and Dean, are you still there?"

"Yes, Dad," they said.

"We're having a major pigeon problem on the roof right now. Your mom and I are trying to work things out with the roof workers, but we'll be here awhile. Can you stay and help Aunt Agnes and Gregory figure this out?"

Dean did a salute even if his dad couldn't see him. "Yes, sir!"

"Stay safe, little mice." Mr. Squeakerton hung up the phone.

Ava was all business. "What happens if we just leave the furniture there?" she asked.

"Then we can't watch what is happening in the Oval Office," Aunt Agnes replied. "More important, we can't get in there. Most Squeakertons only use it as an exercise room, but mice in the Situation Room go into the Oval Office a lot. It's how we stay connected. Sometimes there is top-secret information left on the president's desk that is very useful."

"We don't want this c-a-t anywhere in the West Wing," Gregory said. "It would change our whole schedule. Mice lives are in danger."

"Gregory . . ." Dean looked very serious. His dad told him to help, and Dean listened to his parents. "Are you prepared to serve this mouse country?"

"Aren't you too little to send me on a mission?" Gregory asked.

Ava buttoned Gregory's suit. "Everyone is little next to you, Gregory. We need you to move this furniture. Show this c-a-t that mice are in charge in this house!"

Gregory stood taller. "All right, then."

It was settled. Gregory was going into the Oval Office.

Gregory was a big mouse. So big you might almost think he was a gerbil. He once lifted President Bill Clinton's chair.

Gregory was also a careful mouse. He liked to stay safe. So Gregory insisted on wearing some gear.

He put on a helmet made out of a walnut shell. He took off his suit and put on a black shirt and pants. Ava and Dean wrapped him in bubble wrap. He also wore safety goggles and gloves.

He looked silly, but ready for anything.

Gregory rubbed his hands together. "Assign five helper mice. If I do not return in ten minutes, I want you to send in a team to save me."

"We can't send five mice into the Oval Office!" Aunt Agnes said. "We already have to hide *you*—we can't hide five!"

"How are you going to hide me?" Gregory asked.

Two mice pushed a potted plant into the room.

"Are you kidding?" Gregory asked.

"Do you think humans would rather see a plant moving or a rodent?" Ava asked.

Gregory strapped a camera onto his back.

He easily lifted the plant and held it in front of him. "Fine. I'm ready."

The mice clapped for Gregory as he slipped into a tunnel.

"I hope he's okay," Ava said.

"It's Gregory. He's always okay." Dean put his arm around his sister.

Aunt Agnes turned on the screen. The camera filmed Gregory's movement.

There was a tunnel that led to the president's secretary. Her office was just outside the Oval Office. The door between the offices was still open.

Gregory waited until the secretary left to use the bathroom. He ran out of the mouse hole hidden behind a bookcase. He stayed close to the wall. The plant wobbled in his arms.

"I'm in." He bumped into a chair. Good thing he had on that bubble wrap. The door closed behind him.

The mice watched from the Situation Room. They were very nervous. They could not talk to Gregory through the camera. He could only talk to them.

Gregory set the pot down and faced his mission.

The cat's gym might as well have been a mountain. It was so big compared to Gregory. He pushed. He pushed harder. He pushed hardest. The gym moved, but very, very slowly.

"Come on!" Dean cheered. "You can do this, Gregory!"

The camera shook as Gregory continued to push. Inch by inch, the gym slid across the floor. This was going to take a lot of time and work.

Then the other door of the Oval Office clicked open.

"Oh no!" Ava covered her face with her hands.

Someone was coming into the room! Why would someone come into the room when the president was still giving a tour?

"What do I do?" Gregory squeaked.

But the other Squeakerton mice couldn't

answer him. And Gregory didn't have many choices.

He hurried under a fluffy pillow on the cat bed. Not only was the cat gym blocking their camera and mouse hole, but now Gregory was trapped!

"Thanks for coming to rest with me." The mice had again lost video, but Ava and Dean knew this was Banks's voice. "I think I'm just tired because we were up so late last night at the ball."

"The tour can't go all day." It was a girl's voice. Macey. "Besides, Mom has to do other things besides be a pet owner."

"Whatever. Mom is so proud of Clover. She's like Mom's third kid!" Banks said. "I don't know why we have to stay in the West Wing all day. It's the perfect day to explore!"

"I'm so sad that Clover stays in the Oval

Office now." Macey sighed. "Maybe Mom and Dad will let us get another cat to keep us company."

The mice in the Situation Room groaned.

"Or maybe Clover will have kittens!" Banks said.

The mice groaned even *louder*.

Gregory pushed up the pillow so the camera could film. This was very brave of Gregory.

Banks was sitting on a couch. Macey stood next to him.

"What about those mice we saw?" Banks asked. "I don't want them to get eaten."

"I've never seen Clover eat a mouse," Macey said.

"But she's never been around one. She loves that mouse chew toy," Banks said.

Gregory gulped loudly.

"And she chases anything that moves," Banks added. "She's like a dog."

Macey circled the room. The Oval Office had windows all along one of the walls. The president's desk was built from an old ship. Two flags stood behind the desk. "Clover does like to chase things. She jumps at birds outside. And . . . oh, remember when she ate our betta fish right out of the bowl?"

Banks laughed. "Mom loves her so much. In fact, I bet her first law will be to make sure every American has a cat in their house."

"Is Clover going to sleep here every night or just stay here during the day?" Macey asked. She traced the presidential seal on the rug in the middle of the room with her foot. The seal had an eagle with stars around it in a circle. "Because you know how scared she is of rain and thunder. Actually, any time she gets wet or hears loud noises, she gets mad. We can't leave her in here. Look at these big windows."

"I think Mom wants her in the Oval Office," Banks said. "She said it's about strategy. I don't know what that means."

"I do. But I'm not going to tell you," Macey said.

"Fine. If I see those mice again, I'm not going to tell *you*." Banks folded his arms across his chest.

"I only want to see *those* mice anyway. They were cute. Other mice are gross," Macey said.

Ava and Dean weren't sure if this was a compliment.

Macey ran her fingers along the wallpapered wall. She got bored very easily. "How old is the Oval Office? Do you know?"

Banks shrugged. "I heard Mom saying that President Taft designed it. Then there was a fire in 1929, so they had to rebuild. Before they built the West Wing, all the offices were in the main White House. I'm glad our family has the second floor mostly to ourselves now!"

"So if it's not too old, then there probably aren't as many ghosts in here," Macey said.

Banks froze. "Gh-ghosts?"

Macey nodded at her brother. She was trying not to smile. Ava knew that look. It was the look she gave Dean when she was teasing him. "Oh yes. The president's office has lots of secrets. Ghosts always live with secrets."

Banks pulled his knees up to his chest. "Are you kidding?"

Macey finally smiled. "Maybe I am. But maybe I'm not."

A woman poked her head into the room. "Your mother said to wait in here for a while."

"Why can't we join the tour?" Banks asked. Now that his sister had said there were *ghosts* here, he definitely wanted to leave.

"The West Wing is not a place for children to wander," the woman said. "Your mom said you can join them later."

Macey flopped onto the couch. "We're going to be here all day. Mom will probably be here all night. And then Clover will be here . . . forever."

"So we just have to stay with the ghosts?" Banks asked.

"Oh, stop it," Macey said. "I was just kidding. There aren't any ghosts."

"How do you know?"

"Because then we would see them. Or at least hear them," his sister said. "Now let's see if they have any playing cards in here."

"I wish there were only ghosts," Gregory whispered. "Ghosts leave mice alone! If anyone back in the Situation Room can hear me . . ." Gregory swallowed. He sounded afraid. Ava and Dean had never heard Gregory sound afraid. "I really hope someone has a plan to save me. I'm being held prisoner in the Oval Office!"

"We have to send someone in to save him!" Dean said.

"Who?" Aunt Agnes asked. "They'll get trapped too."

Ava and Dean held tails. They were brave mice. Usually they were smart mice. Gregory always protected them. They would help him now.

"We can fix the Gregory problem," Ava said.

"Yes," Dean said. "Ava and I are the secret weapons."

The mice in the room grumbled. It didn't

seem like they believed little mice could take on such a big job. But Ava and Dean had done something special before. They had so much special in them, and so much more special to do!

Ava smiled. "Remember? Those kids like us. They'll make sure Clover doesn't hurt us. Being small helps us, because we're less scary to the humans. They don't worry about cute little mice like us."

Aunt Agnes jumped up. "That's true! Ava and Dean have already made contact."

The other mice nodded. This was making more sense. "But humans are dangerous too," a mouse said.

"Clover is the danger. Not the kids. We know they won't hurt us," Ava said.

"How would you even *get* to the kids?" Aunt Agnes asked.

That was the problem. The mouse hole was blocked. And the door to the room was closed.

The mice all stared at each other, hoping someone would come up with a plan. After all, the Situation Room was where plans were supposed to happen.

"Maybe we need to move into the Treasure Rooms," Dean said.

"Good idea." Ava slipped on an empty mousepack. "Something in there will help with a plan. I hope."

The mice were very quiet as they marched down the tunnels.

Ava kept thinking about poor Gregory under that pillow. There were probably Secret Service agents outside those doors. They would not let Gregory out of that room alive.

Dean kept thinking about Clover. Was a c-a-t really that bad? The kids were nice to Ava and Dean, and the kids liked Clover. Well, Macey did. Maybe the mice were safe from the c-a-t. Or . . . maybe not.

Twelve mice met in the Treasure Rooms. Ava and Dean were the only kids there.

"Okay, everyone look around," Aunt Agnes said. "See what you can brainstorm. And let's try not to use George W. Bush's toothbrush. I hate touching human toothbrushes."

"Come on, Ava," Dean said. "We have to come up with a plan to save Gregory!"

6

Five items you would find in the Treasure Rooms if you were a mouse and could fit in the Treasure Rooms:

1. Jimmy Carter's nose hair trimmer
2. Michelle Obama's peach-scented soap
3. Lady Bird Johnson's fuzzy bathrobe belt
4. Franklin D. Roosevelt's Q-tip (not used, because EW!)
5. Nancy Reagan's hair spray

Of course, not everything came from a bathroom! The Treasure Rooms really were just a museum of cool stuff the mice had found over the years. There was no section in the Treasure Rooms filled with Stuff to Save Other Mice or Stuff to Get Rid of a Cat. Those would be useful items, though. Probably more useful than a room filled with old buttons.

"What if we never come up with a plan?" Dean asked his sister as he dug through a bin of baby spoons.

"Necessity is the mother of invention," Ava said.

"What does that mean?" Dean asked.

"It means we'll come up with an idea because we have to." Ava touched her scarf collection. "Do you think we can sew this fabric together and parachute into the room?"

"If we had three days, maybe," Dean said. "We don't even have three minutes."

Dean jumped onto a hammer. "Maybe we can build a new mouse hole. I'll need to get a blueprint of the Oval Office. Then I have to figure out a spot that will stay hidden by furniture at all times."

"It's a good idea, but that will take too long. Plus, we don't like to make more mouse holes than we need to," Ava said. "Too bad we don't have a robot dog we can send in to chase after Clover."

Dean tossed some dice onto the floor. "I don't really see Clover being scared of dogs."

Ava froze. "What did you say?"

"I don't see Clover being *scared* of dogs," Dean said. He picked up the dice and rolled them again. "Why?"

A grin spread across Ava's face. "Hold on. I think . . . I think I have a plan." She ran around the rooms until she found two items.

Dean scratched his head. "Huh? Why are you grabbing that stuff?"

"Everyone! Everyone!" Ava called. "I have an idea!"

The mice scrambled into the room with all the kitchen supplies. Aunt Agnes grinned when she saw the items in front of Ava.

"Niece, have I told you lately that you are a very, very smart mouse?"

Ava's plan had some good parts and some bad parts.

The good:

It was a plan. Having a plan is better than
   NOT having a plan.

No one would get hurt. Probably.

There wouldn't be a big mess. Hopefully.

They wouldn't get caught. Maybe.

The bad:

It was dangerous. Likely.

Secret Service agents *did not* like mice.

If the plan didn't work, they had no backup.

"Repeat after me." Aunt Agnes had each mouse raise a hand. "I promise I will not tell anyone about the plan. I promise to do my best to make the plan happen."

The mice said the words with very serious voices even though they didn't know the plan yet. The last time the Squeakertons made a Treasure Rooms oath was when a new tunnel was built under the White House. The workers almost discovered a mouse room. The mice stuck some of the really old Treasure Rooms items in the dirt, and the construction stopped when the workers found the items. Some history people said more items might be buried and the workers could damage them. The mice lost some old things, but at least they kept their mouse room.

That was a close call for the Squeakertons.

"This plan has two parts," Dean said. "First, we will help free Gregory. To do that, we need to get the humans out of the Oval Office. Then . . . then we take care of that c-a-t. Make sure she leaves us alone for good."

Ava smiled at the adult mice. It was fun to be in charge of something like this, even though the reason wasn't good. "The boy, Banks, is scared of ghosts. So we're going to use some Treasure Rooms items to make him think the Oval Office is haunted. Banks is a nice boy, so we'll only spook him a bit. We just need the kids

to leave the room. Clover . . . Clover we'll scare
more. Macey said Clover is scared of thunder,
so we'll make thunder. But first, the kids. Let's
get spooking!"

The mice grabbed what they needed and
marched back to the mouse Situation Room.
Aunt Agnes punched buttons. She moved dials.
"Gregory is hiding under the pillow again. We
can hear what is going on, but we can't see."

She turned up the sound.

"Do you know anything else about the
Oval Office?" Banks asked his sister. "I mean,
besides the g-h-o-s-t-s."

"Mom gets to pick out a new rug soon. It's supposed to look presidential, but I hope she gets purple polka dots instead," Macey said. "I'm sure we'll learn more. Clover will probably learn plenty, living in this room. Too bad we don't have a pet that can talk to us and tell us those things."

Gregory mumbled into the camera, "I know everything there is to know about the White House. But I'm not a pet. I might be Clover's lunch, though, if you guys don't save me soon."

"Gregory is getting cranky," Ava said.

"*Getting* cranky?" Dean asked. "When is he not cranky?"

"Crankier. And scared. We have to do this now," Ava said.

"We're ready when you are," Aunt Agnes said. "Be smart and careful, little mice."

Ava and Dean slipped out of the room and

into the tunnel. They had a large meat hammer that had once belonged to President Eisenhower. Mice are very strong animals. They could have swung that meat hammer alone, but mice don't like to show off.

"Ready?" Dean asked his sister as he lifted her up.

"Go!" Ava said.

Ava swung the meat hammer against a pipe. Metal hit metal. The loud thud echoed in the walls.

"What was that?" Banks asked.

"I have no idea," Macey said.

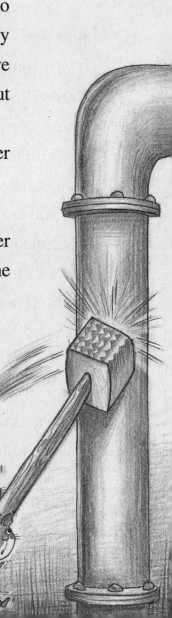

"Harder this time," Dean said.

The mice banged the hammer against the pipe again. They felt this one in their bones!

"It sounds like something is clanging inside the wall," Banks said.

A door opened in the Oval Office.

"Graham, is there someone in the wall?" Banks asked.

Graham was the kids' Secret Service agent. That meant he was in charge of keeping them safe. "There's nothing in the wall," Graham said. "There are agents guarding this room. Always."

"Unless it's a ghost!" Macey said. She sounded scared too.

Ava and Dean nodded at each other. This was a good plan.

"Next step," Ava said. She lifted up a hand-saw with the sharp part pointing away from her.

Dean wobbled the end. This made a moaning sound.

Oooooohhhhh, ooooooohhhhhhhoooohhhhh.

"That is one unhappy ghost," Banks said.

"Maybe you should get out of here. I'll ask your mom if you can join the tour in the Roosevelt Room," Graham said.

"This room is haunted!" Macey said. "Maybe the ghost is from that 1929 fire!"

"I don't care how old the ghost is. I don't want to meet him!" Banks said.

Dean shook the saw again. *Ahaaahhhaaaa.*

"I'm sure it's an—an electrical problem." Graham's voice shook. Ava and Dean had scared an adult human too. Success! "We'll need to send someone in to do a check. We'll . . . we'll wait awhile."

The door clicked shut behind Graham and the kids.

"YAY!" Gregory popped up from under the pillow. The room was empty. Finally!

The mice in the Situation Room watched as Gregory pushed the cat gym out of the way. He really was a strong mouse. More important, he was a very brave mouse.

"Almost . . . there!" Gregory said.

The mouse hole opened. Ava and Dean ran into the Oval Office. Ava gave Gregory a hug.

"How did you do that?" Gregory asked.

"Ava had the idea to bang the meat hammer against a pipe." Dean held out Dwight Eisenhower's meat hammer.

"What about the howling?" Gregory asked.

"Handsaw. I saw it in an old cartoon," Dean said.

"And what about the rattling chains?" Gregory asked.

"What are you talking about?" Ava asked.

"Right at the end. I could hear chains rattling in the room."

Ava and Dean stared at each other. "Um . . . We didn't do that."

Gregory swallowed. "I think it's time we get out of here."

"First, I want to grab something for the Trea- sure Rooms," Dean said.

"Good idea," Ava said. "Who knows when we'll be back? They will probably have a bunch of security guards in here for a while, looking for ghosts!"

"You really didn't make that chain-rattling sound?" Gregory asked, worried.

Dean hopped over the gym, ran around the cat dish, and grabbed something gold.

"A cat hairbrush? Disgusting," Ava said.

"I think it will come in handy for something someday," Dean said.

They slipped back into the mouse hole. The pipe made a whistling sound now. Ava and Dean did not know their own strength! Gregory spoke into his camera. "Agnes, can you send a mouse down here with some chewing gum?

There's a little hole in the pipe that needs to be covered before the whole office floods."

Ava's heart was still pumping from their adventure. They had tricked three humans and saved Gregory! She felt like she could run a million miles.

"What now?" Gregory asked.

"Now . . ." Dean cleared his throat. Being in charge made his voice sound stronger and older. "Now we must stop America from falling in love with that stupid c-a-t."

The Roosevelt Room is a large conference room named after two different presidents: Theodore Roosevelt and Franklin D. Roosevelt. The mice knew that sometimes people got these presidents mixed up because of their same last name. But the mice remembered who Teddy Roosevelt was because he had so many pets. One time, his son Quentin bought some snakes in a pet store. He brought the snakes into the Oval Office during a meeting. He dropped them on the table! Snakes eat mice. Ava and Dean's one-hundredth-great-grandma Mildred almost died that day.

But where were we? Oh yes. The Roosevelt Room. Ava, Dean, Gregory, and his camera slipped through the mouse hole and behind a small chair. They weren't worried about being spotted because so much was happening in the room.

President Caroline Abbey had turned the conference table into a catwalk. A catwalk is another word for a fashion runway. But today there really was a cat walking on the table.

The mice could not believe they almost missed this weird event.

Photographers stood on either side of the table. Clover was modeling a collection of clothes from different time periods. Right now, she had on a fake Abraham Lincoln beard, suit,

and stovepipe top hat. Next she would wear a red ball gown like Nancy Reagan. It was the silliest thing ever to happen in the White House, and that's saying something.

"Who's the designer?" one photographer called out.

President Caroline Abbey beamed. "My husband! Dr. Abbey loves dressing Clover when he's not working."

"I learned to sew in medical school." Dr. Abbey laughed. "I much prefer sewing together a cat jacket to sewing together a heart!"

Banks yawned. It was his first real day living in the White House, and he was already exhausted. Escaping a fake ghost will wear you out. Macey looked tired too. Understandable.

The White House had a movie theater, and instead she had to watch a bearded cat dance on a table.

"Would you ever start your own line of cat clothes?" someone else asked.

"I would love to!" Dr. Abbey said. "We would like to have a fashion show with even more cats from the D.C. area. Clover enjoys having playdates. Maybe we'll make a holiday for cats."

"This has to stop," Ava whispered.

"Right now," her brother agreed.

"Don't worry," Gregory said. "A mouse is going to make sound in the walls soon. The c-a-t will be so afraid!"

The lights in the room darkened for Clover's final outfit. A spotlight shone as she pranced out in a Teddy Roosevelt–style military uniform. Clover even had on little boots!

"Clover Roosevelt! Look over here!" The cameras flashed.

But then there was a loud boom. Then a clap. The photographers stopped snapping.

"The ghost is back!" Banks crawled under the table. Ava and Dean felt bad that he was scared again, but they really had no choice.

Clover froze. Her face went a little white. Which was hard to do, considering her face was covered in orange fur.

A photographer snapped a picture. Another boom shook the room.

"What is that?" Banks asked. "It sounds like thunder."

"And those camera flashes are just like lightning!" Macey said. "Oh no. Clover is going to—"

Clover let out a yowl louder than the boom. Louder than the clap. Louder than any sound known to human ears.

The photographers stepped away.

President Abbey reached for her cat. "It's okay, Clover. It's okay. That isn't thunder."

The sound boomed again.

"What is that noise?" President Abbey asked. "Someone find out now!"

And then . . . and then Clover went crazy. Really, *really* crazy. Crazier than even the mice could have imagined. She scrambled up a wall and knocked over a famous painting. Three Secret Service agents tried to grab her, but she scratched them. She scratched everything and everyone that got in her way.

She even clawed at a pile of wires in the corner. There were spotlights and micro-phones and cameras all set up for the special show. Not anymore. Clover made a pretzel of all the wires!

Secret Service surrounded the president.

"Madam President. We need to remove you. Now."

"But my cat!" she cried. "She's very scared of thunder. She thinks that sound is thunder. What is that sound, anyway?"

"I think our work here is done," Ava said.

"They're going to make four booms," Dean said. "There's still one more."

"I don't want to know what Clover will do if there's another boom," Ava said.

The fourth sound shook the room.

Now Clover jumped onto the table, knocking over the large spotlight. Sparks shot into the crowd. Smoke hissed from the wires.

The smoke detector beeped. Ava and Dean pressed themselves against the wall. The fire sprinklers shot out of the ceiling.

"Oh no!" Macey cried. "Rain! Clover is terrified of rain!"

The photographers covered their cameras with their coats. People rushed out of the room. Clover jumped away from the broken spotlight and started to run in circles. She was acting like a dog! The whole thing was ridiculous.

"Well, I think Operation Scare Clover was a success," Gregory said.

The sprinklers finally stopped.

"We didn't mean to start the water," Ava said. "That poor c-a-t."

Dean shook his finger at his sister. "Don't

pity her. She can still eat us. It's a mouse-eat-mouse world, sister."

"What does that mean?" Ava asked.

"I don't know," Dean said. "I've heard people say it's a 'dog-eat-dog world,' so I tried to change the words. Anyway, remember all that talk of cat holidays and cat playdates. And look, Macey is taking care of her."

Macey wrapped her soaking-wet cat in a sweater. "Clover. Clover. It's okay. That wasn't thunder. Or rain. We just have to get used to the new sounds in our new house."

Clover let out a small meow.

"I know. Let's go

back to my room. I'll dry you off and brush your fur."

The photographers glared at Clover. She did not seem like such a cute cat anymore.

The West Wing was cleared out so the Roosevelt Room could be cleaned. President Abbey called a meeting.

The mice in the Situation Room cheered for Ava and Dean when they entered. They smiled at the rest of the Squeakertons. Both of their tummies hurt a little. It had been a wild, weird day.

Aunt Agnes flipped on the video screen.

"Thank you for staying after that unfortunate event," President Caroline Abbey said to a room full of reporters. "I can assure you, Clover is an amazing cat, as the earlier photos from today will show. There were some loud sounds during her fashion show that sounded like thunder.

Clover is very afraid of thunder and rain. We are already figuring out where that loud noise started."

"Do you think it's a ghost?" one reporter asked.

The president shook her head. "No. There were similar sounds in the Oval Office earlier in the day. We believe it is a pipe or an electrical problem. The West Wing obviously needs to be updated."

Another reporter raised her hand. "Do you still plan on having Clover stay in the Oval Office?"

"I don't think Clover will be in the West Wing again for quite some time." The president brushed a hair from her face. "She needs to recover."

"What is next for you?"

"We have the president of France visiting

this week," President Abbey said. "We need to get to work! I have time for one more question."

A reporter in the front row waved her hand. "Have you ever considered getting a dog instead? Dogs are so fun!"

The president smiled. "We love animals in this family. Maybe we'll get more pets later. But Clover really is a great cat, even if she gets scared sometimes. You'll see."

Aunt Agnes shut off the screen. "Well, we have Gregory back, and Clover won't be in the West Wing for a while. It's back to business for us. Ava and Dean, I think you had some paper airplanes you were going to build today?"

"Really? We're done?" Dean asked.

Gregory saluted them. "Thank you for your service to your country! Now, little mice, go play!"

He didn't need to tell Ava and Dean twice.

They hurried out of the West Wing. All that work had made them hungry. In the kitchen, they each gathered three different cheeses into their mousepacks.

Ava and Dean liked to play in the movie theater. They could listen to any movie that was playing in the background, and they liked dark spaces.

"I just need to drop something off in the Treasure Rooms," Ava said. "Then we can make paper airplanes."

Finally, some nice, relaxing FUN!

They turned the corner and saw something they didn't expect to see.

Especially right outside the Treasure Rooms. Especially when Ava and Dean were all alone. Right now they could use a Gregory. They could definitely use a Gregory.

The Squeakerton mice had a visitor.

"Thanks for the warm welcome today," Clover said. "Now can we have a little chat?"

Just like humans, animals speak different languages. A panda can learn to speak Monkey. A dog can learn to speak Bird. Most animals do not learn other languages, though. Antelopes aren't going to teach their language to lions. The lions would eat them before they could even try.

So it wasn't impossible for a cat to speak Mouse. But it wasn't very common either.

"Chat?" Ava squeaked.

"You know, a talk?" Clover said. "A

conversation? You mice can do that, right? Or is the only way you deal with other animals to bully them?"

"Bully?" Dean asked.

"Are we playing the echo game?" Clover asked. "Yes. Bully. I thought we had a deal. I left you alone last time I saw you. Why didn't you leave me alone today?"

"You chased us last time!" Ava said.

"Yeah. I didn't catch you." Clover licked her paw. She was still wet from the sprinklers. "I had to *pretend* to chase after you. I wouldn't be a good White House cat if I didn't."

"So . . . so you don't want to eat us?" Dean asked.

Clover made a face. "Ew. Gross. No way. I'm a pescatarian."

"Is that a disease?" Ava asked.

"No. It means I don't eat meat. Well, except fish."

Ava and Dean thought it was weird for a cat—any animal, really—to be so picky about food. But right now they were very glad Clover was picky about eating mice.

"We have cheese." Dean scrambled into his mousepack. "Do you want some cheese?"

"Sure." Clover ate all three chunks of cheese in one bite. Her teeth were pointy. Ava and Dean scooted away just in case.

"Thanks," Clover said. "Now, I know there are a whole bunch of mice in here. And I'm fine with that. There were mice in our last house, and I had no problem with them."

Ava smiled and took another step closer to the Treasure Rooms' mouse hole. "Well, great! Glad we have an understanding. We can all live in the same house and get along. I will make sure to tell the rest of the mice."

"Wait." Clover dropped her paw on Ava's tail. "I want my hairbrush back."

"Oh!" Ava glared at her brother. Why did he have to grab Clover's hairbrush? "Um . . . of course . . . I'll . . . I'll go get that for you."

"No way," Clover said. "I'm coming with you."

Ava and Dean blinked at each other. It was great that the c-a-t didn't want to eat them, but the Treasure Rooms were a mouse-only space. Even if they could squeeze Clover in there, they didn't want her to see how big the rooms were. What if she tried to take some things?

"You won't fit," Ava said. "I'll just run in and get it."

"Is this your bedroom in here?" Clover asked.

Ava almost lied, but she did not like doing that. "No. It's another room. There are . . . other things. I'll be back."

Clover yawned. "If there are other things, bring me something else. You guys got all my new outfits wet. You owe me."

She had a point. The outfits were great. Ava would have loved to get some fabric from that Nancy Reagan dress.

"I'll help," Dean said.

Clover stuck her paw on Dean's tail. Tails can be so annoying at times like this. "No. You

stay with me. That way I know your sister will come back."

Dean gulped. "Hurry, Ava."

"Yes, hurry, *Ava*," Clover said.

Ava could have kicked her brother for saying her name in front of the c-a-t. She grabbed the brush right away, but then she didn't know what else to bring. What do you get for a c-a-t as a thank-you present for not eating you?

Then she saw it—the perfect item. The Treasure Rooms had been the answer to all their problems today.

Clover was talking to Dean about presidential fashion when Ava got back. Ava would have loved to talk about fashion. But Dean looked like he was going to faint.

"Here you go." Ava handed the gold brush back to Clover. "And I have another present for you. Actually, it's a present for both of us."

Ava stepped forward and tied a bell around Clover's collar. "The ribbon is green, which is perfect, since you are the president's lucky charm."

"I was before." Clover looked sad. "I don't know if she'll even want me after the mess that happened today."

"Of course she will," Ava said. "Humans love their pets."

"I understand why you want me to wear a bell. Now you can know where I am at all times. Even though, like I told you, I'm not going to eat any of you."

Clover let Dean go. He rubbed his tail.

"I believe you," Ava said. "But the rest of my family might not for a while. So if you can wear this, we'll feel really safe. Plus, everyone who works in the White House will think it's cute. The sound of the bell will be your thing. All divas have something that makes them stand out."

"So . . . my bell will make me a star?" Clover looked excited.

"You live in the White House now. That already makes you the most famous cat in the country."

Clover beamed. She was such a diva.

"So . . . friends?" Dean asked.

Clover grinned. "I didn't say friends. I just said I wouldn't eat you." She strolled down the hallway. "It's a big house. But that doesn't mean I won't have *some* fun. This bell is nice, but you still owe me. I expect you mice to give me the royal treatment while I live in the White House. Or else."

With that, she turned the corner and was gone.

"I really wish the president had a dog," Dean mumbled.

Ava shook her head. They'd had more excitement in the last few days than most mice had in their entire lives. "Be careful what you wish for. You never know what a new president is going to do."

"Like dress her cat like an old president?" Dean asked.

"Exactly." Ava gently nudged her brother

into the Treasure Rooms. "Now let's find some thick paper. I bet my airplane will fly farther than yours."

"No it won't," Dean said.

"Yes it will."

"Will not."

"Will too!"

And then Ava and Dean finally played some mouse games. Which was good, because it wouldn't be too long before they had their next crazy adventure in the White House!

The Presidents of the United States

George Washington
1789–1797

John Adams
1797–1801

Thomas Jefferson
1801–1809

James Madison
1809–1817

James Monroe
1817–1825

John Quincy Adams
1825–1829

Andrew Jackson
1829–1837

Martin Van Buren
1837–1841

William Henry
Harrison
1841

John Tyler
1841–1845

James K. Polk
1845–1849

Zachary Taylor
1849–1850

Millard Fillmore
1850–1853

Franklin Pierce
1853–1857

James Buchanan
1857–1861

Abraham Lincoln
1861–1865

Andrew Johnson
1865–1869

Ulysses S. Grant
1869–1877

Rutherford B. Hayes
1877–1881

James Garfield
1881

Chester A. Arthur
1881–1885

Grover Cleveland
1885–1889

Benjamin Harrison
1889–1893

Grover Cleveland
1893–1897

William McKinley
1897–1901

Theodore Roosevelt
1901–1909

William Howard Taft
1909–1913

Woodrow Wilson
1913–1921

Warren G. Harding
1921–1923

Calvin Coolidge
1923–1929

Herbert Hoover
1929–1933

Franklin D. Roosevelt
1933–1945

Harry S. Truman
1945–1953

Dwight D.
Eisenhower
1953–1961

John F. Kennedy
1961–1963

Lyndon B. Johnson
1963–1969

Richard M. Nixon
1969–1974

Gerald R. Ford
1974–1977

James "Jimmy"
Carter, 1977–1981

Ronald Reagan
1981–1989

George H. W. Bush
1989–1993

William J. "Bill"
Clinton, 1993–2001

George W. Bush
2001–2009

Barack Obama
2009–

Mice Are Smart!

Three (Totally Horrible) Facts
About the Worst Animals Ever

Ugh. C-a-t-s.

1. The first known cat in the White House was Abraham Lincoln's cat, Tabby. Lincoln liked to feed Tabby with a gold fork at White House dinners.

2. Calvin Coolidge's cat, Timmie, was friends with the White House canary, Caruso. Sources say Caruso would walk up and down Timmie's back and even slept between his shoulders. Pretty friendly for a cat.

3. Clover wasn't the first cat to steal the White House spotlight. Bill Clinton's cat, Socks, was (shudder) loved! He appeared on TV shows and in cartoon strips, books, and even a series of stamps in the Central African Republic.

Oval Office: Past

★ Theodore Roosevelt built the West Wing in 1902 so he could work in peace! His kids were always disrupting him in his office. Edith Roosevelt suggested that the second floor of the White House be used only as a home for the president's family.

★ In 1909, William Taft built the first Oval Office, which was damaged by fire on December 24, 1929. Not a great Christmas present.

★ Herbert Hoover added the first phone to the office in 1929. Before that, the presidents used a phone booth down the hall!

★ Lyndon B. Johnson used a green helicopter seat as his desk chair.

★ Ronald Reagan kept jelly beans in the Oval

Office, along with acorns to feed the squirrels outside on the lawn.

★ Franklin D. Roosevelt did not like Americans focusing on his disability. He had a door installed in his desk to cover up his leg braces. This famous picture is of John F. Kennedy Jr. playing in this space.

Oval Office: Present

★ Each president chooses a new rug, as well as art that usually has special meaning. Barack Obama decorated with a bust of Martin Luther King Jr. and a portrait of Abraham Lincoln.

★ An 1823 painting of George Washington hangs above the fireplace.

★ The Swedish ivy on the mantelpiece was

added by John F. Kennedy and has been there ever since.

★ Six of the last eight presidents have used the Resolute desk, which was a gift from Queen Victoria and built out of wood from a ship trapped in Arctic ice.

★ Many presidential addresses are televised from the Oval Office desk. George W. Bush addressed the nation here on the evening of the September 11 attacks.

★ There are four doors in the Oval Office. The east door leads to the Rose Garden—a great escape when the president needs some fresh air!

One lap around the Oval Office equals one mouse mile. Great workout!

The Situation Room

This room is top secret! Read at your own risk.

In April 1961, there was a scary crisis called the Bay of Pigs Invasion, and Presi-

dent John F. Kennedy had a hard time finding real-time information. A month later, the president created the Situation Room. It used to be just one conference room, but in 2007, the space was expanded into three rooms. The Situation

Room hosts up to twenty-five conferences a day, which include up to 250 guests. That's over five thousand visitors a month!

The executive conference rooms' walls have TVs and audio systems hidden inside them. The "surge room" is staffed twenty-four hours a day, seven days a week, with phones and computers always on. The staff receives information about the country and about the world. The president receives daily Situation Room reports in a folder labeled "top secret."

Here's a map showing the West Wing.

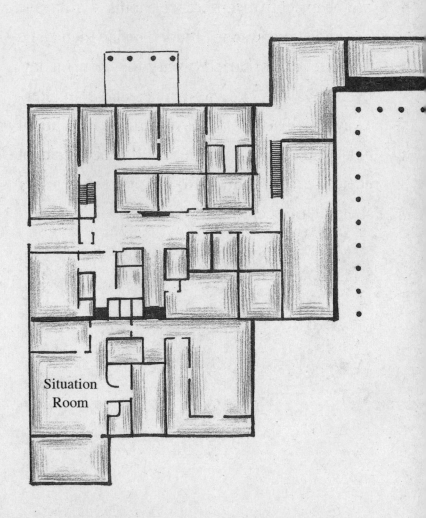

Situation
Room

Mice and humans have Theodore Roosevelt to thank for building the West Wing. Franklin D. Roosevelt also helped—he redesigned the space in 1933. The Roosevelt Room is named after both Roosevelts because of their contributions to the West Wing. There aren't any rooms named after c-a-t-s, because c-a-t-s should *not* be in there. Every mouse knows that!

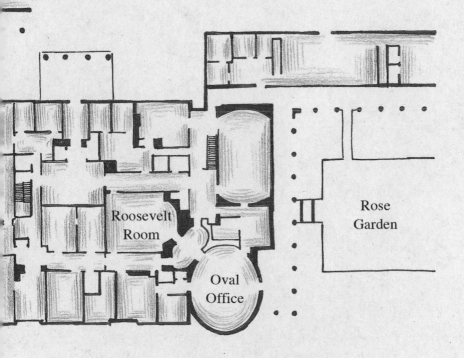

Ava and Dean
are ready for takeoff!
Read on for a sneak peek.

★ ★ ★ ★ ★ ★ ★ ★ ★

Humans think they're the only dreamers in the animal kingdom. This is not true. All animals dream. And not just nighttime dreams—daydreams too. Yes, humans dream about bigger things. They want to ride unicorns or find pots of gold.

Animals are much simpler. Here are some common animal dreams:

1. Dogs dream about fetching a stick.
2. Chickens dream about crossing a road without humans making jokes about it.
3. C-a-t-s dream about ruling the world because they are evil.
4. Pandas dream about bamboo. And more bamboo. And more bamboo.
5. Sloths dream about . . . nothing. Well,

they dream about more sleep. Sloths can
be pretty boring.

Mice are smart animals, and so they have
smart dreams. Ava Squeakerton wanted to do
more than just look for cheese all day. Ava wanted
to fly. For many mice, making this dream come
true would be very hard—mice don't have wings
or money to buy airline tickets.

The Squeakerton family had lived in the
White House for over two hundred years. Ava
and her brother, Dean, knew they were very
lucky to live in such an important building.
There was always food there. They had Gregory, their Secret Service mouse, to look after
them. And they were a part of history!

Ava and Dean were happy little mice.

Still, Ava would sit on the White House roof
and dream her big dream. She could watch the

birds fly overhead, but she never talked to them. Some birds ate mice. She didn't want her first time flying to be in a bird's mouth.

Ava tried to brainstorm ideas with her brother.

"What if we parachuted?" she asked Dean.

"What if we made a trampoline blanket?" she asked Dean.

"What if we rolled around in feathers?" she asked Dean.

What if, what if, what if. None of Ava's plans ever seemed to work. But Ava just wasn't thinking big enough. She didn't need to jump off a building. The most important plane in the world was within her reach.

Air Force One. The president's plane.

Ava and Dean were going to get on that plane. The big question is, would they ever get off?